Marvin Redpost

#6

A Flying Birthday Cake?

by Louis Sachar
illustrated by Amy Wummer

A STEPPING STONE BOOK™
Random House 🏠 New York

To Rachael and Sam

www.randomhouse.com/kids

Library of Congress Cataloging-in-Publication Data

Sachar, Louis, 1954–
Marvin Redpost : a flying birthday cake? / by Louis Sachar.
p. cm.
"A Stepping Stone book."
SUMMARY: Two days after Marvin sees a glowing green thing that looks
like a flying birthday cake in the night sky, his third-grade class is joined
by a mysterious new boy with peculiar behavior.
ISBN 0-679-89000-9 (pbk.). — ISBN 0-679-99000-3 (lib. bdg.)
[1. Extraterrestrial beings—Fiction. 2. Schools—Fiction.] I. Title.
PZ7.S1185Maog 1999 [Fic]—dc21 98-7204

Printed in the United States of America 10 9 8 7 6 5 4 3 2 1
Random House, Inc. New York, Toronto, London, Sydney, Auckland
RANDOM HOUSE and colophon are registered trademarks of Random House, Inc.
A STEPPING STONE BOOK and colophon are trademarks of Random House, Inc.

Contents

1

Seven Minutes After Midnight

It was green.

Marvin stared up at it. He didn't know what it was. He was lying on his back, in a sleeping bag, in Nick Tuffle's backyard.

It glowed as it moved across the night sky.

Nick and Stuart were in sleeping bags beside him. They were asleep.

Today was Nick's birthday. Or maybe that was yesterday. Marvin didn't know if it was after midnight yet.

Seven kids had come to Nick's party,

although only Stuart and Marvin got to sleep over.

But Marvin couldn't sleep. He had eaten too much cake. He had drunk too much punch. The ground was too hard.

He heard a low humming noise. The glowing green thing hovered directly above him. He felt the ground shake beneath him.

He wondered if he was dreaming. It had to be a dream. Maybe he really *had* fallen asleep and didn't know it.

There was a bright flash, then the thing zoomed away. Marvin could no longer see it, hear it, or feel it.

Marvin couldn't fall asleep after that. He stayed up all night, staring at the sky.

At least, he *thought* he stayed up all night. In the morning, he woke up, so he must have fallen asleep sometime. Maybe he was really asleep the whole time.

He remembered that Nick's birthday cake was covered with green icing.

He must have been dreaming, he decided. Now that he thought about it, the green thing had looked like a flying birthday cake. The candles made it glow...

2

A Very Normal Third Grader

Nick's birthday party was on Saturday. On Monday, a new kid came to Marvin's school.

Mrs. North introduced him to the class. "Everybody, this is Joe Normal."

Joe Normal stood at the front of the room, next to Mrs. North. He wore baggy pants, untied sneakers, a Mickey Mouse T-shirt, and a Dallas Cowboys cap.

He looked just like a normal third grader.

"Where are you from, Joe?" asked Mrs. North.

"Uh…Earth," said Joe. "Just like you."

Mrs. North laughed. "Good answer," she said. "But really, what city?"

"City?" asked Joe.

Marvin could tell Joe was nervous. He knew he'd be nervous, too, if he had to move someplace and go to a new school.

"Uh, Chicago," Joe said. "Located on the southwest shore of Lake Michigan, it's the largest city in Illinois."

"What a show-off!" whispered Casey Happleton, the girl who sat next to Marvin.

"Chicago is a beautiful city," said Mrs. North. "I'm surprised you're a Cowboys fan, Joe. I would have guessed you'd like the Bears."

Joe bit his lip and shrugged.

Marvin was surprised Mrs. North knew so much about football.

"Well, it's nice to have you with us," said Mrs. North. "I think you'll like it here."

"Thank you," said Joe. "You seem like a good teacher. I want to learn as much as I can."

Nick groaned loudly.

Mrs. North gave Nick the Look. Then she turned back to Joe and said, "I like your attitude, Joe. Why don't I put you next to Nick? Maybe some of your good attitude will rub off on him."

Nick groaned again.

Nick sat several desks away from Marvin. He turned toward Marvin and whispered something to him, but Marvin couldn't get what he said. It might have been "What a jerk!" or "What a nerd!" He knew it was "What a something!"

Joe sat down next to Nick.

"We've been studying mammals," Mrs. North told Joe. "Who can name a kind of mammal?"

Marvin raised his hand, but Mrs. North called on Casey.

"Bears," said Casey.

That was what Marvin was going to say. He lowered his hand.

Mrs. North continued to call on other children.

"Lions," said Clarence.

"Rabbits," said Heather.

"Humans," said Stuart.

Mrs. North liked that answer. "Very good, Stuart. People are mammals, too. How about you, Joe?"

"Uh, sure, I'm a mammal," said Joe.

Mrs. North smiled. "No, I mean, can you name another kind of mammal?"

"Oh," said Joe. "Um…Oh, I know! What's that one? It's big and fat and has a really long nose…"

"You mean an elephant?" said Nick, beside him.

"That's it!" exclaimed Joe. "I couldn't remember what they were called. Thanks."

"Duh," said Nick.

"That's not nice, Nick," said Mrs.

North. "I'm sure there are times you've forgotten a word."

"I've never forgotten *elephant*," said Nick.

"Well, uh, there aren't a lot of elephants in Chicago," Joe explained.

"Like there are here?" said Nick.

Marvin felt bad for Joe. He knew what it was like to forget a word. Once he couldn't think of the word *parade*.

Mrs. North reminded the class that there would be a test on Wednesday. She asked if anybody had any questions.

Joe raised his hand.

Mrs. North smiled at him. "Yes, Joe?"

"How much does the human brain weigh?"

Mrs. North thought a long time, then said, "That won't be on the test."

3

Wall-ball

A plain concrete wall stood right in the middle of the playground. It wasn't attached to anything.

Sometimes, Marvin wondered who built it, and why. But he didn't complain. Wall-ball was his favorite game.

At recess, he got on line to play.

"I can't believe I have to sit next to Joe!" Nick complained.

"Duh, what's an elephant?" asked Stuart. Then he and Nick cracked up.

"Joe was just nervous because he's new here," said Marvin.

"Duh, how much does my brain weigh?" asked Nick.

Stuart laughed.

"His brain doesn't weigh anything," said Warren, who was in line in front of Stuart. "Because he doesn't have one!"

Marvin looked around to make sure Joe wasn't able to hear them. He saw Joe standing all by himself, on the edge of the blacktop. He looked lost. "Save my place," Marvin said.

He walked over to Joe. "Hi. I'm Marvin."

Joe smiled. "Hello, Marvin. I'm Joe. How do you do?" He held out his hand for Marvin to shake.

"Uh, fine," said Marvin. He shook Joe's hand.

Kids in Chicago were obviously more polite than they were here.

"You want to play wall-ball?" Marvin asked.

"I don't know how," said Joe.

"It's easy," said Marvin. "C'mon."

He led Joe to the wall.

Kenny and Stuart were now playing, and Nick was first in line. Marvin and Joe got on line behind him, and in front of Travis.

"Hey!" said Travis.

"I was here," said Marvin. "Nick saved our places, didn't you, Nick?"

Nick looked at Marvin, then glared at Joe, then looked back at Marvin. "Yeah, I guess," he said.

Marvin knew what he was thinking. He had saved Marvin's place, not Joe's.

Stuart beat Kenny, and now it was Nick's turn.

Nick rubbed his hands together as he

stepped onto the court. "I'm going to kill you, Stuart!" he said.

"Not if I kill you first," said Stuart.

"They're good friends," Marvin assured Joe.

Stuart served. He bounced the big red ball on the ground, then hit it hard with both hands. The ball hit the ground, then the wall, then the ground.

Nick hit it. The ball hit the ground, the wall, then the ground.

"You get how it's played?" Marvin asked.

"I think so," said Joe.

They watched each boy hit it several more times. Then Nick hit his "world-famous cross-court slam," and Stuart was finished.

"Yes, ladies and gentlemen, the mighty Nick Tuffle has done it again," Nick proudly announced. "There is nobody on this planet who can return Nick Tuffle's world-famous cross-court slam!"

"Who's he talking to?" asked Joe.

"The people watching on television at home," said Marvin.

Nick beat Marvin, too, and then it was Joe's turn. "You can do it," Marvin encouraged. He patted Joe on the back as Joe stepped into the court.

Nick served.

Joe hit it back.

Nick hit a long, high bouncer.

Joe jumped up and hit it back.

Nick hit a baby bouncer.

Joe raced forward and got to it before it bounced twice. He was a very fast runner.

Marvin found himself rooting for Joe, even though Nick was one of his best friends.

Nick smashed the return, but Joe ran backward and got to that one, too. He hit the ball off the wall and back to Nick.

Nick was way over on one side of the court when the ball came to him. He was in perfect position. He smashed his world-famous cross-court slam.

Joe raced to it and hit it back.

Nick was still way over on one side of

the court. He couldn't get back to the center in time. The ball bounced past him. Joe won.

When the bell rang, Marvin, Nick, and Stuart headed back to class together.

"I hate Joe," Nick said.

"You're just mad because he beat you at wall-ball," said Stuart.

"I am not," said Nick. "Besides, I would have beaten him, but I wore out my hand beating you and Marvin."

Joe caught up to them, out of breath and smiling. "That was fun!" he exclaimed.

"You ever play wall-ball before?" asked Stuart.

"No, that was my first time."

"Well, no wonder!" Nick exclaimed. "Beginner's luck!"

4

The Door Key

On Tuesday, Joe wore the same clothes he had worn on Monday: Mickey Mouse T-shirt, baggy pants, untied sneakers. But there was one difference. He wore a Chicago Bears cap instead of a Dallas Cowboys cap.

"Good morning, Mrs. North," he said. "I hope I learn a lot today." Then he took his seat next to Nick.

Marvin could practically see the hate coming out of Nick's eyes.

"His name should be Joe Weird, not Joe Normal," said Casey Happleton.

17

"He's just new here, that's all," said Marvin. "You'd probably seem weird, too, if you had to move to Chicago."

"He likes to kiss the flagpole!" said Casey.

Marvin wondered if she was making that up.

"I saw him do it," said Casey. "He just walked right up to it and *kissed* it!"

"Well, maybe that's what they do in Chicago," said Marvin. "Instead of saying the pledge, they kiss the flagpole. He was probably just being patriotic."

"Your name should be Marvin Stupid," said Casey.

Later, at recess, Joe asked Marvin if they were going to play wall-ball again.

"No!" said Nick, before Marvin could

answer.

"Why not?" asked Joe.

"Because it's Tuesday," said Nick. "You can't play wall-ball on Tuesday, can you, Marvin?"

Marvin didn't know what to say.

Just then, two girls from his class, Gina and Heather, came running toward them. They seemed very excited about something.

"Hey, Joe!" said Gina. "Do you know what this is?" She was holding some kind of key.

"It's what you are!" said Heather.

Joe smiled.

"What is it?" asked Gina.

"A key?" said Joe.

"What kind of key?" asked Heather.

Joe didn't know. Neither did Marvin.

"It's a door key," said Gina.

"That's what you are!" Heather exclaimed. "Dorky!"

The two girls laughed.

Nick and Stuart laughed, too. "Dorky!" Nick repeated.

"Don't you get it?" asked Gina. "Door key, dorky?"

Joe didn't say anything.

"He doesn't even get it," said Heather.

Joe walked away. He got it.

"Good. Now that he's gone, let's play wall-ball," said Nick.

"C'mon, Marvin," said Stuart, grabbing him by the arm.

Marvin played wall-ball, but he didn't have any fun. He knew Joe was watching.

5

George Who?

"Why don't you invite Joe to come over this weekend?" suggested Marvin's mother. "He could spend the night."

Two days had passed since Gina and Heather told Joe he was a door key. Now everybody called him that.

Marvin lay in bed. When his mother came in to wish him a good night, he told her about Joe. He didn't tell her everything. He just said he felt bad, because there was a new kid at school and everyone picked on him.

"I try to be nice to him," said Marvin. "I

think he knows that."

Marvin knew what it was like to be picked on. Earlier in the year, everyone had picked on him.

He remembered how bad he felt. It was probably even worse for Joe, he thought, since Joe just moved here from far away.

He wanted to be Joe's friend. But he was afraid that everyone would pick on

him again. And then if Joe moved back to Chicago, Marvin would be friendless.

"I'm afraid if I'm nice to Joe, then the kids will be mean to me, too," he said.

"Maybe if you're nice to Joe, the other kids will be nice to Joe, too," said his mother. She kissed him good night.

On Friday, Mrs. North asked Joe to tell her something about George Washington.

"Who?" asked Joe.

"You, Joe," said Mrs. North.

"I mean, who'd you want to know about?"

"George Washington."

"I don't think I know him."

The class cracked up.

"How about Abraham Lincoln?" asked

Warren. "Do you know him?"

"I don't think so," Joe said. "Does he go to this school?"

Everyone laughed some more.

Mrs. North had to remind the class not to laugh at their classmates. "We go to school to learn. If we already knew everything, then we wouldn't have to go to school."

Marvin didn't laugh. Maybe in Chicago they didn't teach about presidents until the fourth grade.

Joe was still wearing his baggy pants and Mickey Mouse T-shirt. He'd worn the same clothes all week.

"I wonder why he never changes his clothes," Judy said at lunch. "Do you think those are the only clothes he owns?"

She was sitting next to Casey Happleton. Marvin, Nick, and Stuart sat across from them.

"He owns other clothes," said Marvin. "The moving van probably got lost. So he has to wear the same clothes every day, until the moving van gets here."

Joe was sitting all by himself, way down at the end of the table.

"How come you're always sticking up for him?" asked Nick.

"I don't always stick up for him," said Marvin.

"Yes, you do!" said Casey. "When I told you he kissed the flagpole, you said he was being patriotic."

"Do you like him?" asked Judy. "Is he your friend?"

"He's stupid," said Stuart.

"Maybe he knows things we don't

know," said Marvin. "Maybe he knows some really fun games that we've never heard of. Just like he's never heard of wall-ball."

"He's never even heard of *baseball*," said Casey, and everybody except Marvin laughed.

"He's a door key," said Nick.

"Just because he's not from here?" said Marvin. "If you went to Chicago, the kids there might think you were a double door key!"

"That's why I'm not going to Chicago," said Nick.

Judy Jasper had a peanut butter and jelly sandwich and a bag of Cheetos. Marvin watched as she opened up her sandwich. She carefully placed the Cheetos, one at a time, on top of the peanut butter.

The Cheetos fit together like tiles on a bathroom floor.

Stuart had a bag of potato chips. He crumbled the potato chips in his fist and dropped the crumbs into his carton of milk.

"Admit it, Marvin," said Judy. "Joe is just plain weird." She placed the bread with the jelly back on top of the peanut butter and Cheetos.

"He does some pretty strange things," Stuart agreed.

Judy bit into her peanut butter, Cheetos, and jelly sandwich. Stuart drank his potato chip and milk mixture.

"I guess," said Marvin.

6

The Flagpole

After school, Nick and Stuart had to stay inside while Mrs. North talked to them about running in the hallways.

Marvin waited outside. He saw Joe come out of the building and walk down the stairs.

"Hi, Joe," Marvin said.

Joe smiled. "Hi, Marvin."

"So, how's it going?" asked Marvin.

Joe shrugged.

"I guess it's hard being new," said Marvin.

"I guess," said Joe.

Marvin thought about asking Joe if he wanted to come with him to Stuart's house. But he was afraid what Nick or Stuart would say. "Well, maybe it will get better next week. You won't be new anymore."

Joe smiled. "Maybe."

Nick and Stuart came running out of the school building. "We're free!" Nick shouted as he leaped down the stairs.

They stopped short when they noticed that Marvin was talking to Joe.

"C'mon, let's go," said Stuart.

"Where are you going?" asked Joe.

"My house," said Stuart.

Marvin decided to take a chance. "You want to come with us?" he asked.

"Um, I don't know," said Joe. He looked at Stuart.

"You better not," Stuart said. "See, we

have to give my dog a bath."

"That's right," said Nick. "We have to bathe Fluffy. Fluffy is a real mean dog. He might bite you."

"Dogs like me," said Joe.

"It's my parents' rule," explained Stuart. "If Fluffy bites another person, we could get sued for a million dollars! Isn't that right, Marvin?"

Marvin didn't know what to say. He didn't want to lie to Joe, but he also didn't want to betray Nick and Stuart. Besides, if he told Joe the truth, that they really didn't have to bathe Fluffy, it would hurt Joe's feelings.

"And you might get your clothes wet and dirty," said Nick. "You don't want to ruin your *only* clothes, do you?"

He glanced at Stuart and smiled.

Joe shrugged.

"Well, maybe another time," said Marvin.

"Okay," said Joe.

Marvin felt terrible. "See you Monday," he said.

"See you," said Joe.

As they walked away, Stuart said, "I can't believe you asked the Door Key to come home with us."

"I was just trying to be nice," said Marvin.

"Well, you shouldn't just think about yourself," said Nick. "That's selfish. You should think about other people's feelings, too."

Marvin stopped walking. "You're right," he said. He turned around and headed back to the school.

He found Joe standing by the flagpole.

Actually, it looked like Joe was kissing the flagpole.

Maybe Casey Happleton wasn't crazy.

"What are you doing?" Marvin asked.

Joe turned and looked at Marvin. "I was pressing my face against the flagpole."

"Why?" asked Marvin.

"I like the way the cool metal feels when it squashes my nose."

"You weren't kissing the flagpole?" asked Marvin.

"No," said Joe.

Casey Happleton was crazy!

"I decided not to help Stuart and Nick bathe Fluffy," said Marvin. "Do you want to come over to my house?"

Joe smiled and said, "Sure!"

7

Jell-O

"Fluffy wouldn't bite me," Joe said as they walked to Marvin's house. "I've been all over the—well, I've been lots of places. And I've never met a dog who didn't like me. People don't always like me. But their dogs always do."

"Do you have to move around a lot?" asked Marvin.

Joe nodded.

"I guess it's hard to make new friends all the time."

"I don't know what I do wrong," Joe

said. "I try to be like the other kids. But somehow they always know I'm different."

Marvin didn't know what to say.

"It's not all bad," Joe said. "It's fun to get to see all kinds of strange and interesting places."

Marvin never thought that his hometown was strange or interesting.

They came to Marvin's house. There was a fence around his house. The fence was white, except for one red post next to the gate.

"Red post," said Joe. "That's your last name!"

"That's right!" Marvin said, a little surprised that Joe had figured it out. Usually, he had to explain it to his friends. "My dad paints the post once a year."

"Cool," said Joe.

"My mom says she's glad she didn't marry someone whose last name was Purplehouse," said Marvin.

"Why?" asked Joe.

"I don't know," said Marvin. "I think it would be cool to live in a purple house."

"Me, too," said Joe. "Back where I come from, the houses are a lot more colorful than they are here—stripes and polka dots."

"Polka-dot houses?" asked Marvin.

"Sure," said Joe. "Usually, each dot is a different color."

"Boy, I'd like to go to Chicago sometime," said Marvin.

They went inside Marvin's dull gray house.

"Hi, Marvin!" Linzy shouted from the kitchen. She was sitting at the table, eating something out of a bowl.

Marvin set his backpack on the counter. "That's my sister, Linzy," he said. "She's five."

Joe walked to the table. "How do you do, Linzy?" he said. "My name is Joe Normal." He held out his hand.

Linzy giggled and shook his hand.

"What's that red stuff?" asked Joe.

"Jell-O," said Linzy.

Joe stared at it. "What is it?"

"Strawberry," said Linzy.

Joe couldn't take his eyes off of it. "Is it a solid or a liquid?"

"It's Jell-O," said Linzy.

"He's from Chicago," Marvin explained. "I guess they don't eat much Jell-O there."

"Can I touch it?" asked Joe.

"Sure," said Linzy.

Joe poked his finger into Linzy's Jell-O.

"What holds it together?" he asked.

Linzy thought it over. "It's sticky," she explained. "It sticks to itself."

"You want some?" said Marvin.

"I don't know," said Joe.

"It's good. You'll like it," said Linzy.

Marvin opened the refrigerator. He removed a large flat dish filled with strawberry Jell-O. Then he got a small bowl from the cabinet and served some Jell-O to Joe.

Joe sat down next to Linzy. He stared at his Jell-O. He scooped some up on his spoon and watched it jiggle. "It's weird," he said. "I can cut through it with my spoon, like water. But it doesn't fall apart."

"That's because it's sticky," said Linzy.

Joe put some in his mouth. He swished it around and swallowed. "This is deli-

cious!" he exclaimed.

"Told you," said Linzy.

Joe finished his bowl of Jell-O, then ate a second bowlful, and then a third.

"I like Joe," Linzy said to Marvin, while Joe slurped his Jell-O. "He's not like Nick and Stuart. They're weird."

8

Wizzle-fish

"Do you want to call your parents and let them know you're here?" Marvin asked.

"I already told them," said Joe.

Marvin tried to figure out when he could have done that. They'd been together since the flagpole.

The front door opened, and Jacob came home, along with his friend Nate. Marvin was suddenly afraid that Joe might say something that would embarrass him.

Jacob and Nate went to middle school. Marvin admired his older brother. He thought all of his brother's friends were cool, but Nate was the coolest. Usually, Jacob and Nate were nice to Marvin, but sometimes they treated him like he was a stupid little kid.

"Hey, Mar," said Jacob as he tossed his backpack onto a chair.

"Hi," said Marvin. "C'mon, Joe. Let's go up to my room." He wanted to get out of there fast, before Joe said something weird.

"What are you guys doing?" asked Nate.

"Nothing," said Marvin.

"You want to play wizzle-fish?" asked Joe.

Marvin felt himself redden. "They don't want to play," he said. Jacob and Nate never played with Marvin and his friends.

"How do you play?" asked Linzy.

"Everybody needs two wizzles," said Joe.

"But you probably don't have any wizzles."

"No, we don't," said Marvin.

"Paper plates might work," said Joe.

"We have paper plates," said Linzy. "Left over from my birthday, don't we, Jacob?"

"Sure," said Jacob. He went to the pantry and got a small stack of paper plates. "They even have fish on them," he said.

The plates were blue and green and filled with brightly colored fish.

"How do you play?" asked Nate.

Marvin couldn't believe it.

"Here, I'll show you," said Joe.

They went in the backyard to play.

Everyone got two paper plates. They had to try to walk from one end of the yard to the other, stepping only on their plates. It was hard. Marvin had to step on the plate in front of him while he picked up the plate behind him. Then he would toss that plate in front of him and step on it as he picked up the plate he stepped off of.

He was surprised by how much fun it was. Even more surprising, Jacob and Nate had fun, too.

"Why is it called 'wizzle-fish'?" asked Nate.

"Lake Wizzle is a real lake," Joe explained. "Big, flat fish swim around, right at the surface. People try to walk all the way across the lake, stepping only on the wizzle-fish."

"Really?" asked Jacob. "No way!"

"I'd like to try that," said Nate.

"It's dangerous," said Joe. "Sharks swim underneath the wizzle-fish at the bottom of the lake. So if you fall off the wizzle-fish, the sharks will get you."

"Cool," said Jacob.

"And wizzle-fish aren't like paper plates," said Joe. "They move around and wiggle, and are slimy and slippery."

"Have you ever stepped on a *real* wizzle-fish?" asked Linzy.

"Lots of times," said Joe. "But I always stay close to the shore. The sharks are in the middle of the lake."

"What does it feel like to step on a fish?" Linzy asked.

"It tickles a little bit," said Joe.

"You're making this up," said Jacob. "He's making this up, isn't he, Marvin?"

Marvin wasn't sure. Although as far as he knew, sharks didn't live in lakes. Sharks lived only in salt water.

"Where is Lake Wizzle?" asked Nate.

Joe looked up at the sky and said, "Chicago."

Jacob nudged Marvin with his elbow and said, "Your friend Joe is cool. Not like those other two dorks you hang out with."

9

How People Eat Pizza in Chicago

Marvin invited Joe to spend the night.

"Were you born in Chicago, Joe?" Marvin's mother asked him as they sat down for dinner.

"Yes, Nancy," said Joe. "Where were you born?"

For a moment, Marvin's mother didn't answer. Her name was Nancy, but Marvin's other friends always called her Mrs. Redpost. "Richmond, Virginia," she said.

"Where were you born, Dennis?" asked Joe.

"New Jersey," said Marvin's father.

They had pizza and salad for dinner. Since he was a guest, Joe was served first.

Joe used his knife and fork, and cut his pizza into little pieces.

Marvin didn't want Joe to feel weird, so he cut his pizza into tiny pieces, too.

Marvin had warned his parents that the other kids at school made fun of Joe for being different. So when Marvin's mother saw Joe and Marvin cutting their pizza, she did the same.

Marvin's father started to pick up his piece of pizza with his hand. Mrs. Redpost cleared her throat, then said, "Use your fork and knife, dear." Then she cut Linzy's piece of pizza for her. Marvin was glad that Jacob was having dinner at Nate's house. Jacob might not think Joe was cool if he saw him eating pizza. There was no way Jacob would eat pizza with a knife and fork. Jacob sometimes ate two pieces at a time, one in each hand.

"What do your parents do, Joe?" asked Marvin's father.

"Um, just normal things, Dennis," said Joe.

"No, I mean, what kind of work? Did you move here because of their jobs?"

"Sort of," said Joe. "They have a lot of meetings in Washington, D.C. But they were told the schools were better here in Maryland. That's why I'm here."

"What kind of meetings?" asked Marvin's mother.

"I'm not supposed to talk about it," said Joe. "It's top-secret."

"Oh, *I see*," said Marvin's mother.

Marvin saw his parents stare at Joe. He knew they were wondering if Joe was telling the truth.

After they finished the pizza—which took a *lot* longer than usual—Marvin's mother asked what they wanted for dessert. "We've got cookies, ice cream, Jell-O..."

Marvin knew what Joe wanted. "We'll have Jell-O," he said.

Marvin's mother went to the refrigerator. "That's strange," she said. "It's all gone."

"Joe ate it all," said Linzy.

"Can you make more?" asked Marvin.

"That's okay," said Joe. "You don't have to."

"Joe really likes Jell-O," said Linzy. "He'd never had it before."

"They don't have Jell-O in Chicago," said Marvin.

"Oh, *I see*," said Mrs. Redpost. She stared at Joe for a moment. "Well, I can make some more, but it won't be ready until tomorrow."

"Can I help?" asked Joe. "I want to study how you make it."

"Sure, Joe. I'll show you how."

She began by boiling water. "Would you like some cookies for now?" she asked.

"Yes, please," said Marvin.

Linzy said she wanted four cookies.

"How about you, Joe?" asked Marvin's mother.

"No thank you, Nancy. I'll just have a cup of coffee."

10

Floortime

Joe was stirring the yellow Jell-O mixture in a pan on the stove.

"Do you want to call your parents?" Marvin's mother asked him.

"I already did," said Joe.

Marvin didn't know when Joe could have done that.

"If you think Jell-O is good, you should try pudding," said Linzy.

"I feel bad that I haven't even talked to your mother," said Mrs. Redpost.

"She wanted to talk to you, too, Nancy.

But she's in a very important meeting with the president."

"Oh, *I see,*" said Marvin's mother.

Marvin knew his mother didn't quite believe everything Joe said. He wasn't sure he did, either.

"Is there someone at your house who can bring your things over?" his mother asked. "You don't have pajamas, a toothbrush, or a change of clothes for tomorrow."

"I just wear the same clothes every day," Joe said. "I sleep in them, too."

"Oh, *I see.*"

"It's true," Marvin said, sticking up for his friend. "He's worn the same clothes every day for a week."

"And I always take my toothbrush with me wherever I go," Joe said. He reached into the front pocket of his baggy pants

and pulled out a toothbrush.

Marvin's father asked Marvin to help him take the futon up to Marvin's room.

The futon was in the family room. When Nick or Stuart spent the night, they slept on that.

"You don't have to," said Joe. "I'll sleep on the floor."

"The futon is very comfortable,"

Marvin's father assured him. "Just like a bed."

"If you want, you can sleep in my bed, and I'll sleep on the futon," said Marvin.

"I don't like beds," said Joe. "At home I sleep on a hard, flat board."

"Oh, *I see*," said Marvin's mother.

"What should I do?" asked Marvin's father.

"Let him sleep on the floor," said Marvin's mother.

"Can I sleep on the floor, too?" asked Linzy.

A few hours later, Marvin went to bed and Joe went to floor.

"Good night, Joe," said Marvin.

"Good night, Marvin," said Joe. "Thanks for inviting me over. This has been the best day of my whole life."

Marvin was glad. It had been a fun day for him, too. He felt as if he and Joe had been friends for a long time, not just for one day.

"We travel around so much," said Joe. "It's hard for me to make friends."

"I guess the kids at school have been kind of mean to you."

"Oh, they're okay," said Joe. "I've been treated a lot worse. I just wish I knew what I did wrong. I tried so hard this time. Before I came here, I read books and watched movies about what the kids were like here."

Marvin was surprised there were books and movies about that.

"But still, everyone knows I'm different," said Joe. "What did I do wrong?"

"You're not different," Marvin said. "I mean, everyone's different. Life would be boring if everyone was the same."

"But what do I do that is so different?" Joe asked. "I want to fit in. I want the other kids to like me. What do I have to do?"

Marvin didn't know what to say. He didn't want to hurt Joe's feelings.

"I don't want to be a door key," said Joe.

"You're not a door key," said Marvin. "You're a good friend. If the other kids can't see that, then that's their problem."

Marvin hoped he'd said the right thing. He didn't think Joe should have to change. Still, he wondered if maybe he should have told him to change his clothes, at least.

11

Vanished

Joe disappeared.

"Where is he?" Marvin's mother demanded.

"I don't know," said Marvin. "Maybe he walked home."

"I told him I would drive him," said Marvin's mother. "He should know better than to walk home alone."

It was late Saturday morning. Joe had eaten three bowls of Jell-O for breakfast. He played wizzle-fish with Marvin and his family. Even Marvin's mother and father liked playing wizzle-fish.

Then Marvin's mother told Joe to get

his things together, and she would drive him home.

Joe didn't have any things. He just put his toothbrush in his pocket.

Nobody saw him after that.

They looked all over the house for him. Then Marvin and his father got in the car and drove around the neighborhood. Marvin's mother stayed home with Linzy.

"Do you know where he lives?" Marvin's father asked him.

"No," said Marvin, looking out the window. "Don't worry. He's okay."

"Do you know his phone number?" There was a phone in the car.

"No," said Marvin.

Marvin's father called Information and asked for the phone number for somebody named Normal. He spelled it "N-O-R-

M-A-L" and looked to Marvin to make sure that was correct.

Marvin shrugged.

"It's a new listing," his father told the operator. "They just moved here last week...from Chicago."

The operator couldn't find the number.

Marvin's father tried other spellings—"N-O-R-M-E-L-L" and "N-O-R-M-U-L" and "N-U-R-M-A-L." There was no listing.

"It's my fault," Marvin's mother said when they got home. "I should have insisted upon speaking with his parents before I let him spend the night."

"They were in a top-secret meeting with the president," Marvin pointed out.

"Do you really believe that?" asked his father.

"Yes!" Marvin declared. "He's my friend."

"Joe wouldn't lie," said Linzy.

Marvin smiled at his sister.

"I'm just worried about him, that's all," said Marvin's mother. "He never even told his parents he was staying here."

"He said he told them," said Marvin.

"When?" asked his mother. "When did he have a chance to call them?"

Marvin didn't know. "It's not fair!" he exclaimed. "Everybody picks on Joe. First the kids at school, and now my own parents!"

"We're not picking on him. We're trying to help him."

"You think he's a liar!"

"I like Joe, but I'm worried about him. You have to admit that some of the things he does are a bit odd."

"He's my friend," said Marvin.

"I think I better call the police," said Marvin's mother.

Linzy began to cry.

"He's not a criminal!" said Marvin. But despite all his protests, he was worried about Joe, too.

Marvin's mother went to the phone, but just as she reached for it, it rang.

She picked it up. "Hello?"

Marvin saw her face brighten. "Hi, Joe," she said. "We were— You're very welcome. Well, thank you. We enjoyed your visit, too. May I please talk to your mother? Oh, *I see.* Listen, you really shouldn't have—what? Okay, well, bye."

She hung up. "That was Joe. He called to thank us."

"See, I told you everything was okay," said Marvin.

Marvin's mother still looked worried.

12

Wizzle-what?

Monday morning, Marvin left his house carrying a package of paper plates. He tapped the red post for luck as he walked through the gate.

Nick and Stuart were waiting at the corner.

"What are the paper plates for?" asked Stuart.

"Wizzle-fish," said Marvin.

"Wizzle-what?" asked Nick.

"Wizzle-fish. It's a cool game. Joe taught it to me. He spent the night on Friday." Marvin waited to see what his friends would say about that.

"How do you play?" asked Stuart.

Marvin explained it to them. He hoped they'd give it a chance. He hoped all the kids at school would like wizzle-fish. Then maybe they'd like Joe, too.

"You just walk around on plates?" asked Nick.

"Do you try to get anywhere?" asked Stuart.

"It's fun just to walk around," Marvin said. "You only have two plates. If you toss a plate too far away, you're in big trouble. Then the sharks will get you!"

"What sharks?"

Marvin told them about Lake Wizzle, and about the people who try to walk across the lake stepping on big, flat, slimy fish. "Man-eating sharks swim below the fish."

"Let me try," said Stuart.

Marvin gave Stuart two paper plates and watched him try to walk on them. Stuart took two steps, then fell when he reached back to pick up the plate behind him.

Nick laughed. "You're dead. A shark just bit off your head."

Marvin gave Nick two plates and took out two more for himself. The three friends headed to school stepping only on wizzle-fish, while sharks swam around beneath them.

Casey Happleton and Judy Jasper caught up to them.

"What are you doing?" asked Casey.

"Walking on wizzle-fish," said Stuart.

"You are *so* weird, Stuart!" said Judy.

"It's a game Joe taught Marvin," said

Nick. He told the girls about Lake Wizzle. He said that sea monsters lived at the bottom of the lake.

"Can I have a wizzle?" asked Casey.

"You need two," said Nick.

"Me, too," said Judy.

Marvin gave them each two plates. "And by the way, Casey," he said. "Joe doesn't kiss the flagpole. He just likes to press his nose against it. He says it feels good."

"Well, that's how Eskimos kiss," said Judy. "They rub noses."

"That's because it's too cold for Eskimos to kiss on the lips," said Casey. "Their lips would get stuck together."

They walked on wizzles all the way to school. Casey Happleton continued right up to the flagpole. Then she pressed her nose against it. "Joe's right," she announced. "It *does* feel good."

Joe walked into class and took his seat next to Nick.

"Hi, Joe," Nick said. "I was wondering. Have you ever tried playing wizzle-fish tag?"

"No, but it sounds like a good idea."

"You want to try it at recess? Marvin's brought a whole thing of plates."

"Can I play, too, Joe?" asked Gina.

"Me, too," said Heather.

"Sure," said Joe. He turned and smiled at Marvin.

Seventeen kids played wizzle-fish tag at recess. Everyone, including the person who was "It," could only step on wizzles.

There were only twenty-eight plates in

the package Marvin brought to school, so
only fourteen kids got wizzles. The other
three—Clarence, Travis, and Melanie—were
the sea monsters. If anybody fell off a wizzle, a sea monster would grab him or her.

"I can bring more wizzles tomorrow,"
said Nick. "I got a bunch left over from

my birthday party."

"My birthday's on Saturday," said Clarence. "So I'll get my mom to buy lots of paper plates. Hey, Joe, can you come to my birthday party?"

"Sure. I think so," said Joe.

Marvin felt very glad for his friend.

13

At Least

Joe never went to Clarence's birthday party. On Wednesday, Mrs. North announced that Joe would not be returning to class. "His family is having to move again," she said.

Everybody seemed sad, not just Marvin.

"I was just getting to know him," said Stuart.

"Joe is cool," said Travis.

Mrs. North got a big piece of paper and made a giant friendship card for Joe.

At the top it said, *To Joe. Thanks for being our friend.* Beneath that, everyone wrote a short message and signed his or her name.

Marvin wrote, *I hope I get to see you again.*

Mrs. North told the class that she would try to get Joe's address and send the card to him.

Marvin and his friends still played wizzle-fish tag at recess. He noticed that kids from other grades were playing it, too.

He wondered if someday it would be like wall-ball. Nobody knew how wall-ball got started, or why there was a wall in the middle of the playground. Maybe in the future, after Marvin went on to middle school and high school, kids at this school would still be playing wizzle-fish tag. But nobody would know how it got started.

After school, Marvin walked out of the building and slowly down the stairs. It wasn't fair, he thought. The other kids liked Joe now. Why did he have to leave?

He hoped nothing was wrong. Deep down, he'd never quite believed everything Joe told him. What kind of parents would let their child wear the same clothes every single day? What if Joe didn't even *have* parents?

Marvin didn't want to think about it. He pressed his face against the flagpole. The cold smooth metal felt good as it squashed his nose.

Later that evening, Marvin was in his room when Jacob came in and announced, "There's a limousine in the driveway!"

Marvin looked out his window and saw a long, black, shiny car. A soldier stepped out of it. Marvin could see medals and ribbons on his chest. The soldier walked around and opened the back door of the limo.

First a man got out, then a woman, and then Joe.

Marvin and his brother raced down the stairs. They reached the door just as the bell rang.

Joe's eyes were red, like he might have just stopped crying. "Hi, Marvin," he said. "We have to leave."

"I know," said Marvin. "Mrs. North told us. We all wrote you a giant friendship card."

The rest of Marvin's family came to the door. "Hi, Joe," Marvin's mother said brightly.

"Hi, Nancy," said Joe. "These are my parents, John and Jane."

John and Jane said, "How do you do?"

Joe introduced Marvin's family to them. "That's Linzy, Jacob, Nancy, and Dennis. And this is Marvin Redpost, my best friend in the whole universe!"

"Joe told us how much he enjoyed himself the other night," said Joe's mother. "I'm sorry we didn't get a chance to thank you before now, but we were in an important meeting with your president."

"Oh, well, yes, I understand," said Marvin's mother.

"Can I look at the limo?" asked Jacob.

"Of course," said Joe's father.

While Marvin's and Joe's parents continued to talk, Joe led Jacob, Linzy, and Marvin to the limo.

"Cool," said Jacob as he walked around the front of it. The soldier was standing by the back door. "Can I look inside?" Jacob asked him.

The soldier opened the door for him.

Marvin looked inside, too. The backseat was filled with boxes of Jell-O. There must have been over a thousand boxes.

The four adults came over to the limo. Marvin heard his mother ask, "Do you know your new address yet? Maybe Marvin can write to Joe."

"I don't think that would be possible," said Joe's father. "But we'll be coming back this way in two years. We could stop by, and maybe even take Marvin home with us for the summer."

Marvin and Joe smiled at each other. Then Marvin turned to his mother. "Can I?" he asked.

"I don't know," said Marvin's mother.

"Well, in two years you'll be eleven. I guess that will be all right."

"Yes!" exclaimed Joe.

A short while later, everybody said good-bye. Marvin's family stood and waved as the limousine drove away.

Marvin felt sad, but he was glad that Joe stopped to say good-bye. And at least he knew he wasn't saying good-bye forever. It would be fun to go to Joe's house in two years. Maybe he would get to go to Lake Wizzle.

He had been worried, at first, that his mother was going to say he couldn't go. He'd never been away from home for more than a night before, and that was just to Stuart's or Nick's house. Chicago was a long way away, five hundred miles, at least.